angry
cookie

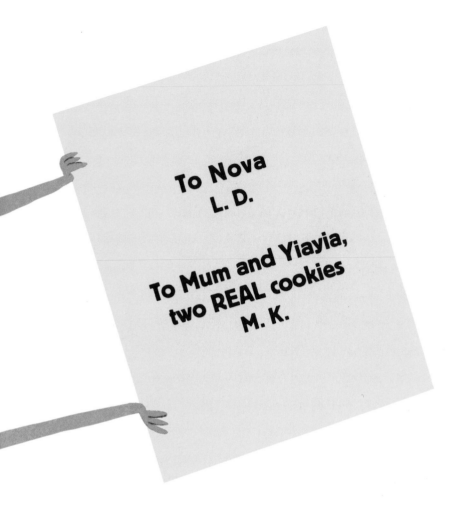

To Nova
L. D.

To Mum and Yiayia,
two REAL cookies
M. K.

First U.S. edition 2019
First published by Walker Books (U.K.) 2018

Library of Congress Catalog Card Number pending
ISBN 978-1-5362-0544-2

LEO 10 9 8 7 6 5 4 3 2 1
18 19 20 21 22 23

Printed in Heshan, Guangdong, China

This book was typeset in Block T Regular.
The illustrations were created digitally.

Walker Books
a division of
Candlewick Press
99 Dover Street
Somerville, Massachusetts 02144

www.walkerbooksus.com

angry cookie

WALKER BOOKS

LAURA DOCKRILL

MARIA KARIPIDOU

AGGGGHH!

It's so bright!
My eyes!

Close this book
this very second,
you nosy
noodle!

The end.

Errr . . . Hellllllooooo!

Ahem.

Cough, cough.

Hint, hint.

Meaning . . .

It all started yesterday
when my roommate, Barbra,
got out her new recorder.
She only knows this one terrible song and
keeps playing it over and over again.

I hate the recorder!

And you're not even allowed to
use the word *hate*.

But I just did,
so there.

But they had run out of the
best, most wonderful
vanilla sundae
with hot caramel sauce
and whipped cream
and marshmallows
and hundreds and thousands
and millions
of chocolate sprinkles
and *even* the red *cherry*.
They did have the tall glass.

On my way home, a bird tried to *snack* on me.
"*Get off! SHOO!*"
I shouted.

But I don't think cookies are *heard.*

Maybe *that's* why I'm so angry at the whole world.

Because *nobody* listens to me. Nobody sticks around.

You keep coming back.